My Little Golden Book About
DINOSAURS

By DENNIS R. SHEALY

Illustrated by STEPH LABERIS

The editors would like to thank Thomas R. Holtz, Jr., Principal Lecturer, Vertebrate Paleontology, University of Maryland, for his assistance in the preparation of this book.

A GOLDEN BOOK • NEW YORK

Educators and librarians, for a variety of teaching tools, visit us at
RHTeachersLibrarians.com
Library of Congress Control Number: 2016930325
ISBN 978-0-385-37861-1 (trade) – ISBN 978-0-375-98224-8 (ebook)
Printed in the United States of America
10 9

Millions of years ago, before people existed, the earth belonged to the dinosaurs.

Some dinosaurs were bigger than a house— and weighed more than a herd of elephants! Others were so small, you could hold them in your hand.

Meat-eating dinosaurs hunted other dinosaurs for food. A predator like Allosaurus had good eyesight and a good sense of smell. It could attack and move quickly.

Allosaurus

Ornitholestes

Other meat-eaters, like Ornitholestes, would scavenge, eating the dead leftovers of other dinosaurs. Yuck!

Apatosaurus

It's possible that Dilophosaurus hunted in small groups. The pair of crests on its skull may have helped pack members identify each other.

Dilophosaurus

Scelidosaurus

Shuvuuia

Smaller dinosaurs, like Shuvuuia, probably
ate lizards and insects.

Other dinosaurs ate plants. These animals weren't defenseless, though. Ankylosaurus was tanklike. Its back was covered with hard, knobby plates for protection. It also had a heavy club at the end of its tail that it could swing at attackers. Watch out!

Ankylosaurus

Stegosaurus, another plant-eater, had a spiked tail to swing at its enemies.

Stegosaurus

Triceratops

Triceratops was a gentle, plant-eating giant with lots of armor. A bony frill protected its neck—and its three sharp horns were perfect for fighting off a Tyrannosaurus rex!

Tyrannosaurus rex

Tyrannosaurus rex was the king of the dinosaurs. It had strong jaws and huge, banana-shaped teeth— perfect for chomping down hard. But it had to be quick to get past other dinosaurs' horns and spikes!

Argentinosaurus had its massive size to keep it safe. The biggest known plant-eater, Argentinosaurus must have had to eat all the time. It was longer than three school buses and weighed more than thirteen elephants!

Amazingly, all dinosaurs—big or small—hatched from eggs.

Argentinosaurus

Giganotosaurus

Huge creatures also swam in the seas and flew in the sky. Mosasaurus and Elasmosaurus were reptiles—like lizards and snakes—that hunted fish and squid.

The neck of an Elasmosaurus was about 25 feet long. That's four times longer than a giraffe's neck!

Mosasaurus

Elasmosaurus

Quetzalcoatlus

Pteranodon

Flying reptiles like Pteranodon had wide wings made of skin that stretched between their long, skinny arms and short back legs. The biggest flying reptile was Quetzalcoatlus. Its wingspan was larger than our smallest fighter jet!

What happened to the mighty dinosaurs? Scientists think that an asteroid—a giant piece of space rock and metal—hit the earth. The explosion sent dust and ash flying into the air, turning the skies dark for a very long time.

Without sunlight, plant life couldn't have survived.
Soon there wouldn't have been enough food for most
dinosaurs—especially the biggest ones.

Luckily, the dinosaurs left fossils behind. Fossils are bones or teeth or footprints, buried in clay or sand, that hardened into rock over time. Scientists carefully dig them up to study. They also put fossil skeletons back together, like a puzzle, so you can see them in museums.

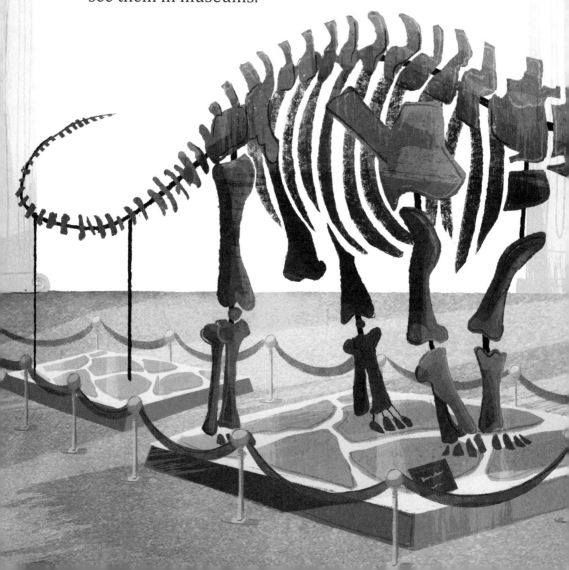

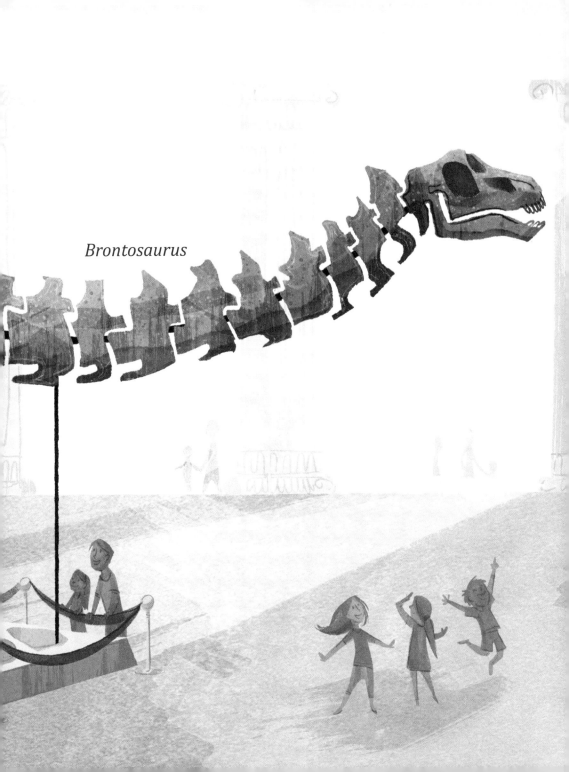

Brontosaurus

One of the most surprising fossils found so far is the Archaeopteryx—a small dinosaur with feathers! Since it was discovered, scientists have found many other fossils that reveal that different types of dinosaurs had fuzz or feathers.

Archaeopteryx

Now scientists think that some dinosaurs—
the ones that walked on two legs—looked like . . .

...*birds!*

Velociraptor

Deinonychus

Caudipteryx

Fossils show us that the skeletons of these dinosaurs are similar to the skeletons of birds. Like birds, these dinosaurs have S-shaped necks and wishbones in their chests. In fact, scientists now believe that birds are the living relatives of the dinosaurs that didn't die out.

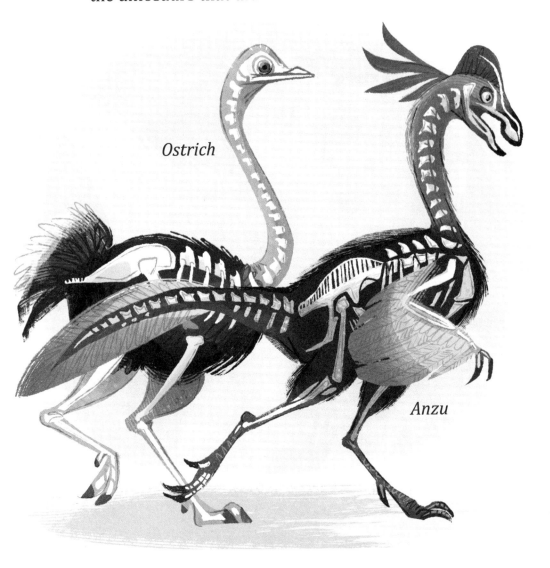

Ostrich

Anzu

The big dinosaurs became extinct long ago, but isn't it exciting to know that living, flying dinosaurs—*birds*—are all around us?